W9-BYF-915

PARKER DRESSES UP

by **Parker Curry & Jessica Curry**
illustrated by **Brittany Jackson & Tajaé Keith**

Ready-to-Read

Simon Spotlight

New York   London   Toronto   Sydney   New Delhi

For my surgeon, Dr. Mudd
—P. C.

For all the little ones dreaming of who
they'll become in the future!
—J. C.

SIMON SPOTLIGHT
An imprint of Simon & Schuster Children's Publishing Division
1230 Avenue of the Americas, New York, New York 10020
This Simon Spotlight edition January 2022
Text copyright © 2022 by Parker Curry and Jessica Curry
Cover illustrations copyright © 2021, 2022 by Brittany Jackson
Interior illustrations copyright © 2022 by Brittany Jackson
For information about special discounts for bulk purchases, please contact
Simon & Schuster Special Sales at 1-866-506-1949 or business@simonandschuster.com.
Manufactured in the United States of America 1221 LAK
2 4 6 8 10 9 7 5 3 1
Library of Congress Cataloging-in-Publication Data
Names: Curry, Parker, author. | Curry, Jessica, author. | Jackson, Bea, 1986-
illustrator. | Keith, Tajaé, illustrator.
Title: Parker dresses up / by Parker Curry & Jessica Curry ; cover illustrations by
Brittany Jackson ; interior illustrations by Tajaé Keith.
Description: Simon Spotlight edition. | New York : Simon Spotlight, 2022. |
Summary: While playing dress-up, Parker and her siblings imagine endless
possibilities for future careers. Identifiers: LCCN 2021019956 (print) | LCCN
2021019957 (ebook) | ISBN 9781665902557 (paperback) | ISBN 9781665902564
(hardcover) | ISBN 9781665902571 (ebook) Subjects: CYAC: Costume—Fiction. |
Occupations—Fiction. | Brothers and sisters—Fiction. | Curry, Parker—Childhood
and youth—Fiction. | African Americans—Fiction. | LCGFT: Picture books.
Classification: LCC PZ7.1.C8665 Pan 2021 (print) | LCC PZ7.1.C8665 (ebook) |
DDC [E]—dc23
LC record available at https://lccn.loc.gov/2021019956
LC ebook record available at https://lccn.loc.gov/2021019957

My name is Parker.
I love to play outside.
But today it is raining.

Then I get an idea.
I can play dress-up!

My little sister and brother want to play too.

"I am a queen!"
says Ava.
Cash waves a magic wand.

I pull on a tutu.
Then I close my eyes.

I pretend I am a ballerina.
"Bravo!" cheers the crowd.

Next I put on
a white coat.

I pretend
I am a doctor.
I can make anyone
feel better!

Then I hear a screech.
"No, Cash!" yells Ava.
"Cooks do not use hoses!"

The hose lands on my doll.
"Hey!" I yell.

Cash starts to cry.

My mom enters the room.
"What is wrong?"
she asks.

"Cooks do not use hoses,"
Ava says.

"Firefighters do not
bother doctors,"
I say.

"Can a cook also be a firefighter?" my mom asks Ava.

Then she asks me,
"Can a doctor also be
a forgiving sister?"

"Everyone can be
more than one thing,"
my mom says.

"Just look at me!
I am a mom and a writer."

"Look!" Cash says.
He is wearing
a new costume.

Now he is
a superhero builder!

I put on a new costume too.
I dress up as
a mermaid teacher.

Ava dresses up as
a fairy artist.

"Playing dress-up
is the best thing
in the world!" Ava says.

"President Parker
does not agree,"
I say.

"It is the best thing in the whole universe!"

MAKING FASHION WAVES

Do you like playing dress-up like Parker? What are your favorite clothes and costumes to wear? Here are a few people who grew up to become famous fashion designers.

TRACY REESE is an American fashion designer who started her own clothing label in 1998. Many people have worn her designs, including Oprah Winfrey, Tracee Ellis Ross, Meghan Markle, and Michelle Obama! In 2019, Tracy created Hope for Flowers. The clothes in the Hope for Flowers line use sustainable materials that are better for the environment.

CHRISTOPHER JOHN ROGERS is an American fashion designer. Although he's still at the beginning of his career, he has already won many major awards! He also designed the outfit Vice President Kamala Harris wore on Inauguration Day when she was sworn in as the first Black American, the first South Asian American, and the first woman vice president of the United States of America.

STELLA JEAN (say: JOHN) was born in Rome, Italy. She was a model before becoming a fashion designer. Stella tried out twice for a famous Italian fashion contest, but she was rejected both times. She didn't give up, though. On her third try, she won second place. Many of Stella's designs are inspired by her Haitian and Italian background.

If you could design new clothes or accessories, what would they look like? Try drawing your ideas in a sketchbook!